BLESSINGS and PRAYERS for LITTLE BEARS

BLESSINGS and PRAYERS for LITTLE BEARS

Linda Hill Griffith

HarperCollinsPublishers

With blessings and prayers

for my husband Bob and

our daughter Lauren

L.H.G.

God has made the world
So broad and grand,
Filled with blessings
From His hand.
He made the sky
So high and blue,
And all the little children, too!

UNKNOWN

All things bright and beautiful,
All creatures great and small,
All things wise and wonderful,
The Lord God made them all.

Each little flower that opens,
Each little bird that sings,
He made their glowing colors,
He made their tiny wings. . . .

The tall trees by the greenwood,
The meadows where we play,
The rushes by the water,
We gather every day.

He gave us eyes to see them,
And lips that we might tell
How great is God Almighty,
Who has made all things well.

CECIL FRANCES ALEXANDER

For this new morning with its light,
Father, we thank Thee,
For the rest and shelter of the night,
Father, we thank Thee,
For health and food, for love and friends,
For everything Thy goodness sends,
Father in heaven, we thank Thee.

RALPH WALDO EMERSON

The kiss of the sun for pardon,
   The song of the birds for mirth,
One is nearer God's Heart in a garden
   Than anywhere else on earth.

DOROTHY FRANCES GURNEY

God, make my life a little light,
   Within the world to glow;
A little flame that burneth bright,
   Wherever I may go.

God, make my life a little flower,
   That giveth joy to all,
Content to bloom in a native bower,
   Although the place be small.

God, make my life a little song,
   That comforteth the sad,
That helpeth others to be strong,
   And makes the singer glad.

Matilda Betham-Edwards

Thank you for the world so sweet,
Thank you for the food we eat,
Thank you for the birds that sing,
Thank you, God, for everything!

EDITH RUTTER LEATHAM

Now I lay me down to sleep,
I pray the Lord my soul to keep.
Thy love be with me through the night,
And keep me safe till morning light.

UNKNOWN

Peace be to this house
And to all who dwell in it.
Peace be to them that enter
And to them that depart.

Unknown

He prayeth best, who loveth best
All things both great and small;
For the dear God who loveth us,
He made and loveth all.

SAMUEL TAYLOR COLERIDGE

Angel of God, my guardian dear,
To whom God's love commits me here;
Ever this day be at my side
To light, to guard, to rule and guide.

UNKNOWN

Dear Father, hear and bless
Thy beasts and singing birds,
And guard with tenderness
Small things that have no words.

UNKNOWN

I see the moon,
    And the moon sees me;
God bless the moon,
    And God bless me.

UNKNOWN